TO: BROOKSTON

Love

Mimi &
PAPA

MCMUNK

MR. MCMUNK

PEANUT

SAM

Better Together!

by **Amy Robach** and **Andrew Shue**

Illustrated by **Lenny Wen**

FLAMINGO BOOKS

One stormy night, the wind howled through the woods, the trees shook, the branches clacked, and . . .

Mrs. Squirrelly and her two little squirrels
were blown right out of their nest!

"This way!" Mrs. Squirrelly called. "I know a hollow tree nearby."

Beck and Fern followed their mama through the forest to an oak tree with a hollow trunk. It was warm and dry inside.

Meanwhile, not far away, the wind was howling, trees shaking, branches clacking, the rain coming down and down and down, and . . .

swiiiiish!

Mr. McMunk and his two little chipmunks were blown right out of their burrow!

"Follow me," Mr. McMunk called to Peanut and Sam. They followed their papa to the hollow in the trunk of a great oak. It was warm and dry inside . . .

and full of squirrels!

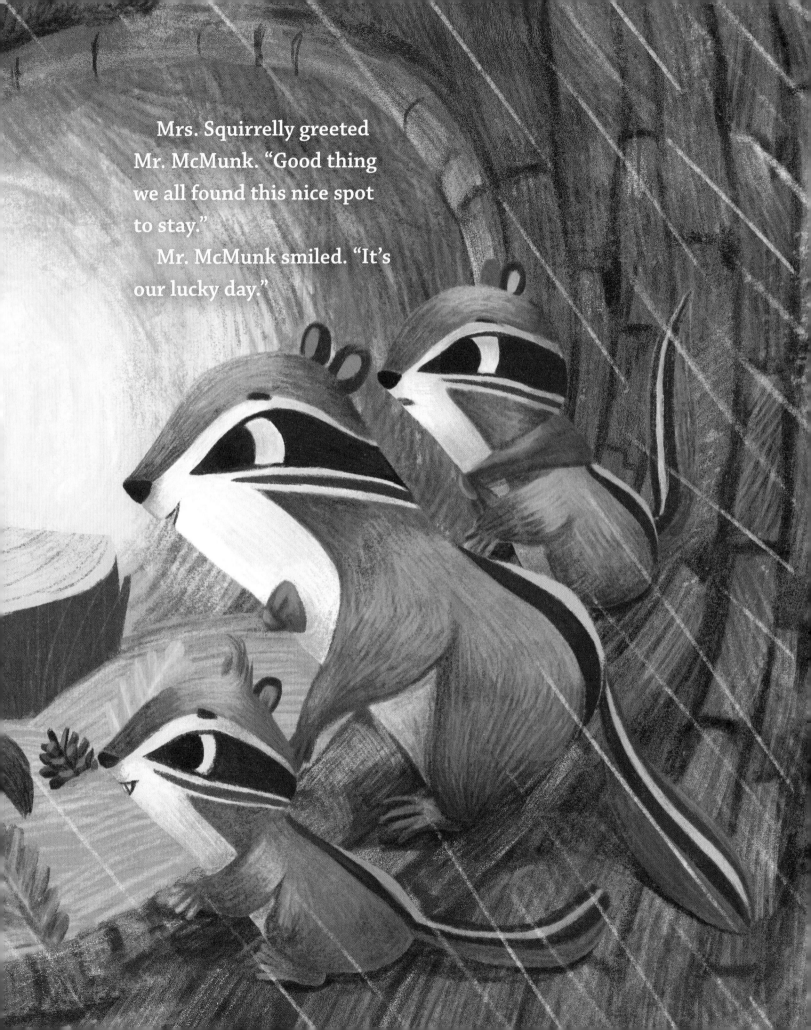

Mrs. Squirrelly greeted
Mr. McMunk. "Good thing
we all found this nice spot
to stay."

Mr. McMunk smiled. "It's
our lucky day."

Beck and Fern and Sam and Peanut were shy at first. But not for long.
A full hollow meant there was always someone to play with.

Beck loved Stack the Sticks, and it turned out Peanut did too!

Sam was a huge fan of Rotten Nut Hunter—and so was Fern!

Plus some games just were paws-down better.

Jumping rope with two was tough. But with four? No problem!

Fern and Beck and Sam and Peanut played Tree Trivia.

And Nutball.

And tag.

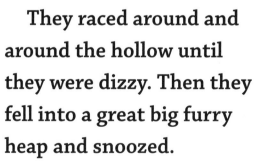

They raced around and around the hollow until they were dizzy. Then they fell into a great big furry heap and snoozed.

The storm raged all night and
into the next day. The wind kept
blowing. The rain kept falling.
After a while, everyone got
a little testy.

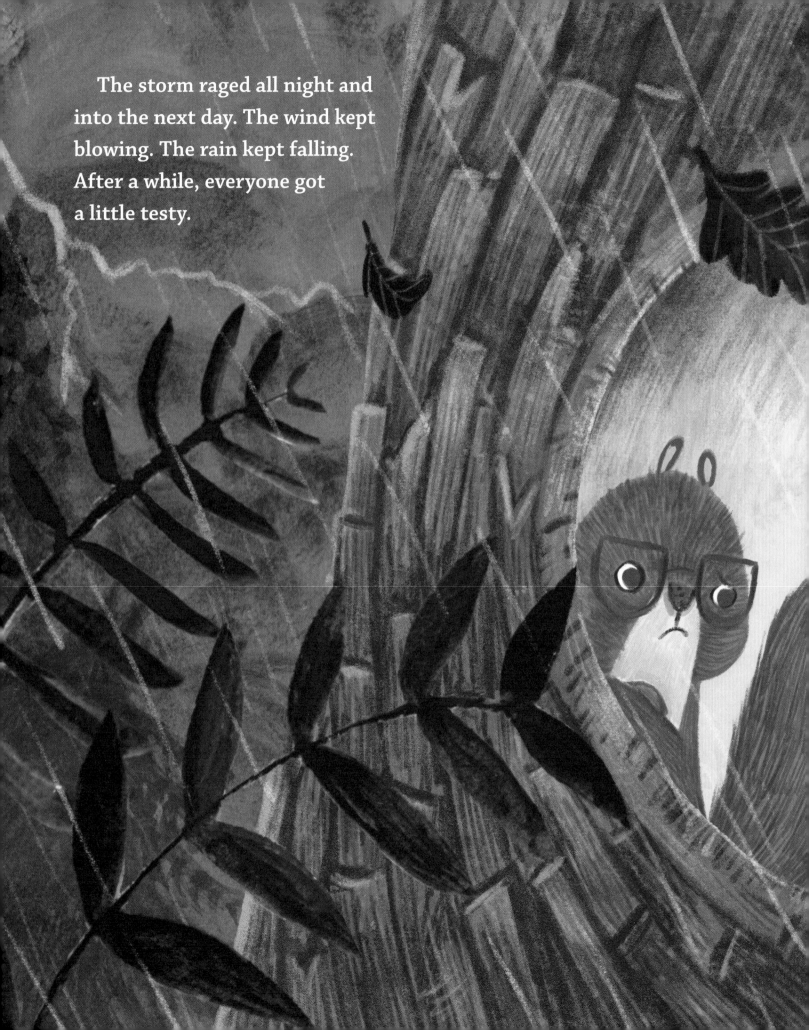

"Quit poking me with your paw," Sam told Fern.
"You're hogging all the pine needles!"
Beck complained to Peanut.

After a long night, Mr. McMunk made breakfast.
"How about some mushrooms?" he asked.

Beck wrinkled her nose. "In our nest, we always eat berries for breakfast."

"Beck! Don't be rude," Mrs. Squirrelly said, as she set out acorn caps full of rainwater.

"Rainwater?" Peanut crossed his paws.

"In our burrow, we drink dewdrops."

Mr. McMunk sent him to the corner.

The grumping got worse.

Almost everyone wanted things to go back to the way they were before the storm.

"Our nest was the best," Fern said.

"Our burrow was awesome," said Peanut.

"Why do we have to share?" Beck wailed.

"All they ever do is chatter," Sam said.

"Chatter, chatter, chatter."

"We do not!" Beck shouted.

"Do, too!" Peanut yelled back.

Mrs. Squirrelly threw up her paws.
"Enough! From now on, squirrels will stay
in this part of the hollow."

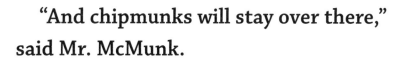

"And chipmunks will stay over there,"
said Mr. McMunk.
Peanut and Sam and Mr. McMunk went
to one side.

Fern and Beck and Mrs. Squirrelly went to the other.
Just as they settled in, Beck looked outside and . . .

"The storm is over!" she cried.

"We can go home!" Peanut added.

So Mrs. Squirrelly took Fern and Beck back to their nest at the top of the tree. Mr. McMunk took Peanut and Sam back to their burrow.

But what they had thought was the best and awesome wasn't quite how they had remembered it.

The nest had a great view, but it was a little drafty.

The burrow was super cozy,
but a little damp.
Most of all, both felt too quiet.

And empty.

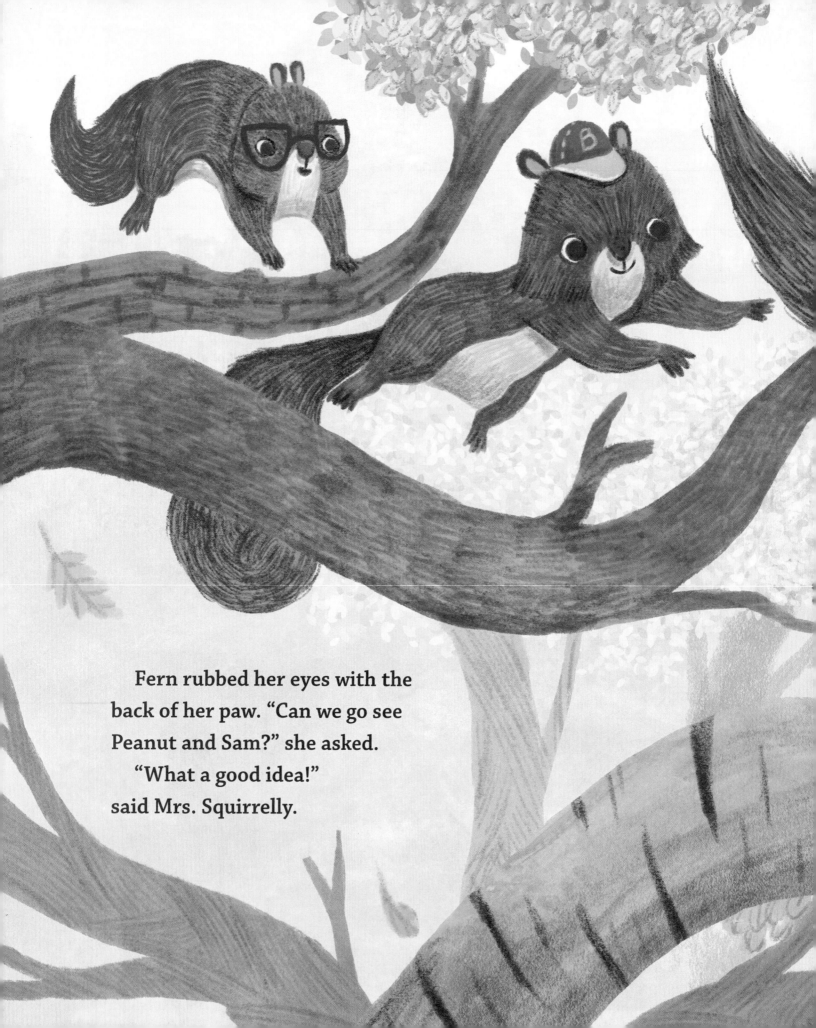

Fern rubbed her eyes with the back of her paw. "Can we go see Peanut and Sam?" she asked.

"What a good idea!" said Mrs. Squirrelly.

Meanwhile, Peanut found berries tucked away in a corner of the hollow. "Beck and Fern would really like these," he said. "They always eat berries for breakfast."

"Let's take some to them!" Sam said.

So Peanut and Sam and Mr. McMunk
raced out of the burrow and climbed up
the oak tree just as Fern and Beck and
Mama Squirrel were climbing down.
They met in the middle . . .
by the hollow.

The squirrels and chipmunks raced circles
around the tree when they saw each other.

"Mama, can we stay here from now on?" Fern begged.

"Us, too?" Sam and Peanut asked their papa.

"We'll see," said Mr. McMunk. He smiled at Mrs. Squirrelly.

"I think I'll try mushrooms for breakfast tomorrow," Beck said.

"No, let's have berries," said Peanut. "With rainwater."

"Deal," said Sam and Fern. They all shook paws.

And that's how the squirrel and chipmunk families became the McSquirrelies.

Together.

For good.

We dedicate this book to our children—Nate, Aidan, Ava, Wyatt, and Annalise—
who proved that family is defined not by blood, but by love. —A.R. & A.S.

For Anaëlle and Melvyn, who accepted me with open arms
and have brightened my days ever since. —L.W.

FLAMINGO BOOKS
An imprint of Penguin Random House LLC, New York

First published in the United States of America by Flamingo Books, an imprint of Penguin Random House LLC, 2021

Visit us online at penguinrandomhouse.com.

Library of Congress Cataloging-in-Publication Data is available.

Manufactured in China

ISBN 9780593205693

1 3 5 7 9 10 8 6 4 2

RRD
Design by Kate Renner and Lucia Baez
Text set in Chaparral Pro

The art for this picture book was created digitally in Photoshop with pen display
and layered with scanned traditional mixed-media textures.